d Care

Stone Arch Readers are designe
experiences, as well as opportu
literacy skills, and comprehen:
support your beginning reader.

- Talk with your child about the ideas addressed
  in the story.

- Discuss each illustration, mentioning the characters,
  where they are, and what they are doing.

- Read with expression, pointing to each word. You may
  want to read the whole story through and then revisit
  parts of the story to ensure that the meanings of words
  or phrases are understood.

- Talk about why the character did what he or she did
  and what your child would do in that situation.

- Help your child connect with characters and events
  in the story.

Remember, reading with your child
should be fun, not forced. Each
moment spent reading with your
child is a priceless investment in
his or her literacy life.

Gail Saunders-Smith, Ph.D.

STONE ARCH **READERS**

are published by Stone Arch Books, a Capstone Imprint
151 Good Counsel Drive, P.O. Box 669
Mankato, Minnesota 56002
www.capstonepub.com

Library of Congress Cataloging-in-Publication data
is available on the Library of Congress website.
ISBN: 978-1-4342-2053-0 (library binding)
ISBN: 978-1-4342-2795-9 (paperback)

Summary: Kayla's cat, Daisy, is missing. Kayla is very worried.
She calls her friends, and soon enough the entire Pet Club is on the case.

Reading Consultants:
Gail Saunders-Smith, Ph.D.
Melinda Melton Crow, M.Ed.
Laurie K. Holland, Media Specialist

Art Director: Kay Fraser
Designer: Emily Harris
Production Specialist: Michelle Biedscheid

Find the CAT!

A
PET CLUB
STORY

by Gwendolyn Hooks
illustrated by Mike Bryne

STONE ARCH BOOKS
a capstone imprint

Lucy, Jake, Kayla, and Andy are best friends. Lucy has a rat named Ajax. Jake has a dog named Buddy.

Kayla has a cat named Daisy.
Andy has a fish named Nibbles.
Together, they are the Pet Club!

Every day, Kayla comes home
from school at the same time.
Every day, Daisy is waiting.

But today, Kayla comes home
early. Daisy is not there!

Kayla looks everywhere. She looks inside.

She looks outside. Kayla can't
find Daisy!

Kayla calls the Pet Club.

Her friends say they will be
right over.

"I brought Buddy," Jake says.

sniff

sniff

"He can track Daisy's smell," Kayla says.

"I brought Ajax," Lucy says.

"He can look in small spaces,"
Kayla says.

"I brought Nibbles," says Andy.

"Nibbles is Daisy's best friend,"
Kayla says.

"Let's get to work," Kayla says.

Buddy sniffs Daisy's dress-up clothes.

Buddy sniffs and sniffs. Then he runs to the kitchen. Jake and Kayla follow him.

"Oh no! Buddy ate Daisy's food," Kayla says.

"Buddy does love to eat," Jake says.

After eating, Buddy runs off
again. He sniffs every room
in the house. No Daisy.

Ajax checks every small hiding
place in the house.

No Daisy.

Nibbles starts blowing lots of
bubbles. She swims in fast circles.

She even jumps out of her bowl!

"What is it, Nibbles?" Andy asks.

"Look!" Kayla says. "It's Daisy!"

Kayla checks her watch.

"I came home early today.
But Daisy is right on time!"
she says.

"What time is it?" Jake asks.

"Time to get more food for
Daisy," Kayla says.

STORY WORDS

school	smell	house
early	friend	clothes
track	sniffs	kitchen

Total Word Count: 256

Join the Pet Club today!

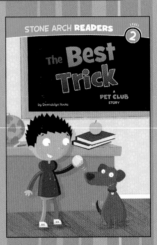